![Disney]

PIRATES of the CARIBBEAN
ON STRANGER TIDES

Adapted by James Ponti

Based on the screenplay by Ted Elliott & Terry Rossio

Suggested by the novel by Tim Powers

ased on characters created by Ted Elliott & Terry Rossio and Stuart Beattie and Jay Wolpert

Based on Walt Disney's Pirates of the Caribbean

Produced by Jerry Bruckheimer

Directed by Rob Marshall

DISNEP PRESS
New York

Prologue

"DEAD MEN TELL NO TALES."

That was the warning pirates offered those who braved the seas. But one man seemed to defy that rule with great regularity. Captain Jack Sparrow had been left for dead more times than he could remember. He had been stranded on deserted islands, sentenced to eternity in Davy Jones's Locker, and sucked beneath the surface of the ocean by the bloodthirsty Kraken. Each time he was doomed, with no chance of survival. Yet, somehow, he always managed to return to the living with stories of great adventure.

So, sometimes, dead men—or at least men who were supposed to be dead—did tell tales.

But none could equal this particular tale—the one told by a Spanish sailor who was lost at sea for nearly two hundred years. He was pulled from the ocean by a fisherman as the last moments of sunset cast a faint orange glow across the dark waters of the Atlantic. . . .

CREE-YAK! wailed the winch as the fisherman turned the crank that lifted his net from the sea. *CREE-YAK!* Against the darkening sky he could faintly make out a shape; something was trapped in the net. *CREE-YAK!* He continued to turn the crank and study the shape until his worst fears were realized. *CREE-YAK!* There among the fish trying to escape was the body of an ancient sailor.

"Captain!" called the fisherman. "Captain!"

The captain arrived just as the sailor's lifeless body spilled out onto the deck.

Both said a quick prayer as they looked down on the poor lost soul. The old man's clothes were tattered and torn; twisting strands of seaweed were wrapped around his arms and legs; and water poured from his long white beard. Remarkably, a book remained securely wedged between his chest and arm. When the captain reached down to get it, the most amazing thing happened.

The ancient sailor opened his eyes.

Although he could barely whisper a few halting words at a time, the sailor told them what turned out to be an incredible story, a story, he insisted, that the king needed to hear. They agreed, sailed straight for the royal city of Cadiz, and took the old man to the palace. Because the sailor was too weak to walk, they had to carry him in a worn canvas sail.

King Ferdinand was the opposite of the ancient man who lay dying on the floor of the palace. The old and feeble sailor was undoubtedly of humble origins, his greatest achievement his service to the crown. Ferdinand, however, was young and privileged, said to be divinely chosen by God to lead the Spanish people. And now, through the words of this man, Ferdinand thought he might be able to achieve what his forefathers only dreamed of—immortality. He studied the sailor, who barely clung to life as he strained to take shallow breaths while still managing to keep a tight grip on his book.

The captain of the fishing boat spoke first. "We believe he's found . . ."

The king held up his hand to silence him. He wanted to hear it from the sailor himself. He kneeled down next to the ancient man, who struggled to open his eyes.

With a wheeze that seemed to drain all his energy, the sailor said, "Ponce de Leon."

King Ferdinand nodded and looked over his shoulder at a mysterious man whose skin had been darkened by a lifetime spent sailing the seas. They shared a knowing look, and then the king turned back to the ancient sailor. He took the book from the sailor's tight grasp and saw that it was an old ship's log from the *Santiago*. The king began to carefully turn the pages.

"He says he's found Ponce de Leon's ship," the captain explained.

"Or sailed on it," the fisherman added.

"No," the captain snapped, not wanting to sound ridiculous in front of the king. "I told you, Ponce de Leon died two hundred years ago."

"But he died searching for something," the fisherman responded, not backing down.

King Ferdinand nodded. He knew exactly what Ponce de Leon had searched for centuries earlier. And here in the ship's log he saw a symbol that could mean only one thing.

"The Fountain of Youth," Ferdinand said.

His mission complete, the sailor flashed a faint smile and spent his final breath, easing into a death that had long awaited him.

The king stood and turned to the mysterious man.

"How soon can you sail?" he asked as he handed him the old ship's log.

The mysterious man did not hesitate to answer.

"With the tide."

Chapter One

"HURRY PAPA, OR WE'LL MISS THE HANGING," a little girl said excitedly as she raced down a crowded cobblestoned street. "They've caught a real pirate! I want to see."

She wasn't the only one.

Beneath a dreary gray sky, a crowd of Londoners poured into the Old Bailey, which is what they called their courthouse. They came to see the trial—and probably the hanging—of an infamous pirate. The courtroom was filled to overflowing, and the crowd greeted the prisoner with boos and hisses as the jailer led him in, his wrists and ankles bound in manacles, a black hood covering his head.

The bailiff stood up and read the indictment. "Now appearing before the court, the notorious pirate, brigand, pillager, and highwayman, Captain Jack Sparrow!"

More boos and hisses rained down at the sound of his name. Jack Sparrow was a hated man, his reputation well-known throughout London. But while most of the people in the courtroom had heard stories of his evil deeds, apparently none of them had ever seen him. Because when the jailer pulled off the prisoner's hood, no one realized that it was somebody else.

"I told you the name is Gibbs," the man pleaded. "Joshamee Gibbs!"

Joshamee Gibbs was a pirate. And he often sailed as Jack Sparrow's first mate. Somehow he had been mistaken for his boss, and now an angry mob was screaming for his blood. With no way to prove differently, a show of mercy from the court— which seemed unlikely to say the least—was his only hope of avoiding hanging.

"Hear ye, hear ye," the bailiff continued. "Commencing now, the sessions of the peace. Presiding over these trials, the highly esteemed magistrate of South York. All rise for the Right Honorable Justice Smith!"

The crowd shouted as the judge sauntered into the room, wearing his black robe and a large, white powdered wig. He also held a lace handkerchief in front of his mouth, making it difficult for the people who jammed the courtroom to get a good look at his face.

He dropped the handkerchief just long enough for Joshamee to get a glimpse of the glint in his eye and the flash of gold in his mouth. Gibbs instantly recognized him. It was Jack Sparrow, apparently adding "impersonating a judge" to his long list of crimes and misdemeanors.

"Jack?" Gibbs said, disbelieving. The bailiff jabbed him in the gut with a billy club.

"Not necessarily," said the judge, who was really Jack. "You were saying?"

"Jack . . . Sparrow is not my name," the prisoner claimed. "My name is Joshamee Gibbs."

"Is that so?" Jack asked with a wry smile. "It says Jack Sparrow here."

"I was making inquiries as to the whereabouts of Jack Sparrow," Gibbs tried to explain. "Who I'd learned had come to London. And who I would be happy to identify to the court if it would help my case."

He shot his friend a look, and Jack quickly tried to change the subject.

Jack turned to the jury. "The prisoner claims to be innocent of being Jack Sparrow. How do you find?"

The foreman of the jury didn't know what to say. They hadn't even had a trial yet.

"Foreman!" Jack said forcefully. "Your finding? Guilty?"

"Guilty verdict means he'll hang," the foreman responded.

"Yes," said Jack, bringing a round of cheers from the crowd.

The foreman scratched his head, unsure how to render a verdict without a trial. "Guilty?"

Another cheer from the gallery.

"That's not fair," pleaded Gibbs.

"Not favorable to you," Jack corrected. "But fair is not the same as favorable. You have been found guilty and so are sentenced to hang."

The people roared their approval and began to stomp their feet in anticipation of the hanging. Jack banged his gavel to silence them. He was a master of double-talk and was now about to use it against the assembled mob.

"What say you?" he asked the crowd. "You want me to set this prisoner free?"

A chorus of nos and calls to kill him rang through the courtroom. The judge was clearly mistaken. The crowd wanted this man to hang.

"I cannot in good conscience set this man free," Jack said, continuing his double-talk. "Joshamee Gibbs, the crime of which you have been found guilty is of being innocent of being Jack Sparrow.

5

I hereby sentence you to be imprisoned for the remainder of your miserable life."

Slowly the people in the gallery began to realize that there would be no hanging.

Jack turned to the bailiff. "Arrange to transport this prisoner to the Tower of London."

The mob began to boo and hiss, and some people threw old fruit and garbage. Jack pounded his gavel just as a shoe flew past his head.

"Stop," he commanded. "Order, order, you hooligans. Restore order."

More objects flew toward him, and Jack decided it was time to get out of the courthouse.

"Court is in recess!" he proclaimed with a healthy wallop of his gavel before throwing a shoe and some garbage back at the gallery. Then he rushed out the back just as a riot was beginning to erupt.

As he raced down the hallway, the pirate quickly transformed from stodgy Justice Smith back into swaggering Captain Jack. He ripped off the wig and robe and tossed them into a closet, where the actual judge sat bound and gagged.

By the time he stepped outside, Jack looked like his old familiar self—knee-high sea boots, a striped sash around his waist, and a red bandana on his head. All that was missing was his tricorn hat, which he plucked off the head of a horse that was hitched to a paddy wagon. It was the same paddy wagon he'd just commanded the bailiff to use to take Joshamee Gibbs to the Tower of London.

Jack winked at the driver, who flashed him a sly smile. The driver reached for the reins and in the process exposed the skull-and-bones tattoo on his arm. Everything was going exactly as planned.

Jack walked around to the rear of the wagon, where the guard took him for a prisoner and tossed him in the back alongside his old first mate.

"Crikey!" said Gibbs upon seeing his friend. "Now we're both off to prison."

Jack flashed his gold-filled smile. "Not to worry, I've paid off the driver," he assured him. "In ten minutes we should be outside of London town, horses waiting. Tonight we make for the coast. Then it's just a matter of finding a ship."

Now Gibbs was the one smiling. The driver snapped the reins, and the horse started pulling the wagon across the cobblestoned street.

"What happened, Gibbs?" Jack asked as he offered his flask of whisky to his friend. "I thought you had another gig."

"Aye, but I always listened like a thief for news of the *Black Pearl*," he said as he took a sip and handed the flask back to Jack. "No one's seen hide nor hair of it. And then I hear a rumor, Jack Sparrow's in London."

"Am not," Jack said, wondering how the rumor got started.

"But that's what I heard," Joshamee replied. "Jack Sparrow's in London with a ship and looking for a crew. Fact is, you're signing men tonight at a pub called the Captain's Daughter."

"Am not!" Jack protested, getting more confused.

Gibbs nodded. "I thought it a bit odd. But then you've never been the most predictable of sorts."

Jack mulled this over for a moment. "Truth is, Jack Sparrow arrived in town just this morning to rescue Joshamee Gibbs from one appointment with the gallows."

Gibbs smiled. "Like I said, unpredictable."

Jack did not like this one bit. "So there's another Jack Sparrow out there, sullying my good name."

"An impostor," Gibbs said.

"Aye," Jack answered and then added, "an impostor with a ship."

There was a glint in his eye that Gibbs knew well. It seemed that Jack Sparrow was once again a captain in need of a ship, and he was always willing to do almost anything to get one.

Jack put the cork back in his flask and slipped it into the inside pocket of his jacket. Gibbs noticed a rolled-up map tucked in there as well.

"What about you?" he asked Jack. "Last I heard you were bent to find the Fountain of Youth. Any luck?" For centuries, no destination had proven more tempting nor elusive than the mysterious Fountain.

Jack gave a wry smile as he pulled out his map and showed it to Gibbs. "Circumstances arose and forced a compelling insight regarding discretion and valor."

"Meaning you gave up," the first mate replied with a chuckle.

"So untrue," he assured him. "I am just as bent as ever. I'll taste those waters. Mark my words."

Joshamee Gibbs slapped his friend on the shoulder. "There's the Jack I know."

Jack nodded confidently. "And I'll not have it said there's a point on the map Captain Sparrow never found."

It was just like Jack to speak so confidently while locked in the back of a paddy wagon. He had it all planned out. Or at least he thought he did. Just then the wagon came to a sudden stop. Jack frowned. They couldn't have made it outside of London so quickly.

"Short trip," Jack said as he slipped the map back into his coat pocket.

The door to the wagon opened. Jack and Gibbs climbed out and found that they were now in the courtyard of St. James's Palace, home of the king and certainly not where Jack had arranged to go.

They looked around and saw that the king's royal guard had them surrounded, their rifles trained on them.

"All part of the plan?" Joshamee asked.

Before Jack could answer, the captain of the guard slammed him in the head with the stock of his gun. Jack crumpled into Gibbs's arms before falling to the ground. Another guard shoved Gibbs back into the paddy wagon and slammed the door shut.

A woozy Jack looked up as the wagon pulled away. He was finally able to answer Joshamee's question, but it was too late.

"No," he said.

Chapter Two

As a man who favored dirty saloons an dank, dark pirate ships, Jack Sparrow was more than a little out of place as he was marched through the elegant hallways of St. James's Palace. And, though he was in the custody of two guards and under the very real threat of winding up at the gallows, he couldn't help but salivate at the fact of so much royal treasure, just waiting to be plundered, nearby.

As was their tradition, the royal guards did not say a word as they went about their duties, making it impossible for Jack's fast talking to get him out of trouble. They led him into a dining room with ornate furnishings, including impossibly long drapes and a massive chandelier. They shoved him into a hard wooden chair and chained him to its arms. He knew it was useless to protest so he tried a smile, which, of course, got absolutely no reaction from the guards. Once he was fully secured, they left the room and locked the door.

When he looked at what lay before him, Jack began to salivate again. Because, in addition to all the priceless art and antique furniture, the room had a long dining table that held a sumptuous array of mouthwatering food. The smell alone was intoxicating. His only "meal" that day had come from his whiskey flask, and Jack's stomach started growling. He strained to break free from the chair.

The table was just beyond his reach, so he tried to move his chair closer to it. After a few bounces he was almost there. He stretched out his fingers, craned his neck, and practically wished the food into his gaping mouth. But he was still too far away.

If he could not move closer to the food, he

decided to see if he could move the food closer to him. He leaned back in the chair and kicked the bottom of the table. A cream puff bounced off its plate and rolled toward him. Jack's eyes widened. This could work.

He kicked the table again, and the cream puff rolled even closer. The plan was working; Jack could practically taste the pastry. After another kick, it was hanging over the edge of the table. Now, it would only take one more nudge.

Jack carefully placed the toe of his boot under the edge of the table, but just when he went to flick it, the door flew open and a column of royal guards marched in. Startled, Jack fell back and accidentally kicked too hard. The cream puff flew high into the air and landed right in the middle of the chandelier.

Jack sat there with a slightly broken heart and a very empty stomach. With the guards in the room, there was no way he could try again. The guards were followed by a host of servants and various advisers to the king. The final person to enter was none other than King George himself. The king plopped his considerable girth into a chair at the opposite end of the table and instantly began devouring the feast that Jack so desperately craved. Jack couldn't help but notice that the dashing military hero portrayed in the mural on the wall bore little resemblance to the fat man stuffing his face at the end of the table. As with pirates, sometimes reputation and reality were two different things.

"I've heard of you," the king said as he munched on a thick piece of meat.

Jack couldn't help but feel pride at the fact the king had heard of him.

"And you know who I am," George continued.

"The face seems familiar," Jack answered slyly.

The king's prime minister bellowed, "You are in the presence of George Augustus, Duke of Brunswick-Lunenburg, arch-treasurer and prince-elector of the Holy Roman Empire, King of Great Britain and Ireland." The man gave Jack a sideways look before adding, "And of you."

Jack smiled. "Doesn't ring a bell."

George gnawed a chunk off a giant turkey leg. "I am informed that you have come to London to procure a crew for your ship."

"Vicious rumors," Jack said. "Not true." As he talked, Jack rattled his chains, making an annoying racket.

"I'm quite certain that's what my minister told me," the king replied in midchew. "'Jack Sparrow has come to London to procure a crew.'"

"It may be true that that's what you were told," Jack said, rattling his chains some more. "But it's nonetheless false that I have come to London to procure a crew."

King George stopped eating momentarily and studied Jack. "Then you lied to me when you told me you were Jack Sparrow."

"No, no. I am Jack Sparrow. And I am in London. But I am not here to procure a crew. That is someone else."

"Ah," George said, finally getting it. He turned to

his guards. "You've brought me the wrong wastrel. Find Jack Sparrow and dispose of this impostor."

Two guards moved toward him, and Jack held up his hands for them to stop.

"Wait! I am Jack Sparrow. The one and only." He continued rattling his chains louder and louder, and the noise was getting on King George's nerves. "And I am in London."

"To procure a crew to undertake a voyage to the Fountain of Youth?" the king continued. He had finally had enough of the rattling, and he turned to the line of guards. "Someone, remove those chains."

This was exactly what Jack had wanted all along.

A guard came over and unhooked the chains, and Jack smiled at his newfound freedom. Yes, he was still in the middle of the king's palace surrounded by rifle-toting guards, but to Jack Sparrow these were minor obstacles. The chains had been the real hindrance.

The king took a deep breath and decided to try

one last time. "At the risk of repeating myself—Jack Sparrow is in London recruiting a crew to return to the Fountain of Youth?"

"Stipulated," Jack said, rising from his chair. He was desperate to grab a piece of food before the king ate it all.

"Have you a map?" asked the king.

Jack reached into his jacket pocket and, much to his surprise, the map was not there. He wasn't sure where it had gone, but he was relieved that the king's men wouldn't get it.

"No," he said.

"Where is it?" demanded the prime minister.

"The truth? I lost it. Quite recently, in fact." In his mind he raced through what had happened after he'd shown the map to Joshamee Gibbs. All that he could figure was that Gibbs had somehow lifted it when they were in the paddy wagon. Part of him was disappointed that Gibbs would steal from him, but another part was impressed that he had lifted it so well.

George selected a loaf of bread from the table. "I have a report. Trustworthy. The Spanish have located the Fountain of Youth." He started to angrily tear the loaf into small chunks. "I will not have some melancholy Spanish monarch gain eternal life!" He continued shredding the bread and pounded it into flat little pieces. "I trust my demonstration has been clear."

Jack raised an eyebrow. "You've clearly demonstrated something."

With the king momentarily flustered, his prime minister stepped forward.

"You do know the way to the Fountain?"

Jack nodded. "Absolutely. Yes!"

"And you could lead an expedition?"

Jack was feeling more confident by the moment. Suddenly he was of value. He moved his chair closer, sat down, and propped his feet up on a corner of the table. "You'll be providing a crew and a ship?" he said, smiling.

"And a captain," added the king.

Jack's smile disappeared. He thought he would be the captain.

"We believe we have found just the man for the job," the minister said.

He motioned to a guard, who opened the door. Jack sat upright and heard footsteps approaching. Actually it was a footstep followed by a longer scraping sound. Then another footstep followed by another long scrape. This pattern continued until the shadowy captain emerged from the darkness, his tall frame filling the doorway.

He wore a Royal Navy officer's hat but the coat of a privateer, which meant he was a private person who captained a ship with the same authority and power as a true military official. He leaned on a crutch and his right leg was wooden from the knee down, which explained the long scraping noise when he walked. And while the clothes and peg leg were new, the face was one that Jack had known for years. It was that of his longtime nemesis, Hector Barbossa.

"Why is that man not in chains?" Barbossa demanded as he continued step-scraping into the dining hall. "He must be manacled at once."

"At the center of my palace?" scoffed the king with a laugh. "Hardly."

"Jack Sparrow be easy enough to catch," Barbossa warned. "It's holding him that's the problem."

"Hector," Jack said with a friendly boom, hoping to direct the conversation away from the topic of chaining him again. "Good to see a pirate make something of himself."

"Privateer," corrected Barbossa. "On a sanctioned mission, under the authority and protection of the crown."

Jack quickly got to the point that most interested him. He wanted to know about the ship that both of them had captained. "What became of the *Pearl*?"

"Lost her," Barbossa said with true remorse in his voice. "Lost the *Pearl*. Lost my leg. I be genuine contrite on both counts."

Jack arched an eyebrow. "Lost?"

"I defended her mightily, but she be sunk, none-theless."

There was one unbreakable rule of pirates and naval officers alike. So it didn't sit well with Jack that the ship he loved dearly had sunk, yet its captain had not gone down with it. He lunged toward Barbossa only to be held back by two guards.

"If that ship be lost properly," Jack said, face-to-face with Barbossa, "you should be lost with her."

"Aye," Hector said softly. "In a kinder world."

The guards now had their rifles trained on Jack's head. He stepped back.

"Captain Barbossa," interrupted the king. "Has our situation not been made clear? Each second we tarry, the Spanish outdistance us. I have every confidence you will prevail and be rewarded with the high station you desire."

Barbossa turned to the king and bowed.

Jack could not believe his eyes, a dread pirate like

Hector Barbossa bowing to a fat king munching on a turkey leg. "You, sir, have stooped."

Barbossa shook his head in disagreement. "Jack, our sands be all but run. Where's the harm in joining the winning side? Shorter hours, better pay. You meet a nicer class of person. And, it's clean."

"But, Hector," Jack said, still shaking his head, "the hat."

He motioned toward Barbossa's prim and proper hat, and when the guards looked at it as well, they were distracted just long enough for Jack to make his move. He grabbed the guards and slammed them together. Their rifles fired, bullets hitting the massive chandelier. A rope snapped, and the chandelier started swinging wildly.

The room in sudden chaos, the guards first moved to block the door. But that wasn't where Jack was headed. Instead, he jumped up on the table, ran along it, and leaped onto the chandelier just as it swung past. Flying above the heads of the guards, Jack flung himself up to a second-floor balcony in an amazing gymnastic maneuver. As if that wasn't enough, he managed to pluck the cream puff from the chandelier as he went.

He popped the cream puff into his mouth and gave a quick wave before disappearing through a second-story window. The guards stood momentarily frozen, dumbfounded by Jack's brazen move. After a moment they chased after him, but it was too late. He ran along a rooftop, jumped over the castle gate, and quickly disappeared into the crowded London streets.

"He escaped," King George said, disbelieving but still eating.

Just then the chandelier crashed down in the center of the table, and Hector Barbossa resisted the urge to say, "I told you so." Instead, he offered, "Round one to Jack Sparrow."

Chapter Three

JACK SPARROW DIDN'T MUCH CARE FOR London. He'd been there for less than a day and already had King George, the prime minister, Hector Barbossa, a high-ranking judge, and a large portion of the population wanting him to hang from the gallows. And, while a lifetime of pirating had certainly earned him a dubious reputation, it seemed that someone posing as Jack Sparrow was going around town making matters worse.

And the weather was awful, too.

So, as a dark and dreary London sky became a darker and drearier London night, Jack headed for the wharf to find a pub called the Captain's

Daughter. When they were in the back of the paddy wagon, Joshamee Gibbs had said the impostor Jack was supposed to recruit his crew there. The real Jack figured that if he made a surprise visit to the pub he might be able to get to the bottom of things.

The Captain's Daughter was loud and dirty and had a foul stench about it. It was filled with ruffians, highwaymen, and would-be pirates, who all seemed on the verge of breaking into fights for no particular reason. In other words, Jack felt right at home when he walked through the doors. This was certainly a much better fit for him than the Old Bailey courthouse or St. James's Palace.

He surveyed the scene and quickly set his gaze on a line of sailors. They were waiting by a door to a warehouse at the rear of the pub. The door was guarded by a beefy sailor who sat on a stool and strummed a mandolin to pass the time. One at a time he'd let the next in line enter the warehouse. Jack bumped into an old salt drinking ale and asked him what was going on in back.

"Those folks over there," said the old sailor as he took another swig from his tankard, "they have a ship and are looking for able hands."

Jack winked at the old man and disappeared into the crowd.

Scrum was the name of the sailor playing the mandolin, and he was quite skilled at it. He finished a song with an impressive flourish and half expected a round of applause from those in line. Instead, the only response he got was a knife pressed against his throat.

Jack had come up from behind and now held the tip of his blade against the young man's Adam's apple. "I hear you be recruiting a crew," Jack whispered in his ear.

"Aye," answered Scrum, carefully trying not to move his Adam's apple as he spoke. "That is, Jack Sparrow be putting together a modest venture."

"Don't you know who I am?" Jack asked.

Scrum let out a nervous laugh. "Hey! Here's a bloke what forgot his own name!"

Just then the door to the warehouse opened, and a young pirate burst out with a happy smile on his face. He'd just signed on with who he thought was the famous Captain Jack Sparrow. "I'm in, boys!" he said to the others in line. "Who'll buy a sailor a drink?" The pirates in line congratulated him and slapped him on the back.

Jack looked through the still open door and spied a shadow on the far wall. He tilted his head, not sure what to make of the fact that this shadow looked exactly like his own.

Slipping past Scrum and into the room, he could hardly believe what he found: standing in front of him was none other than Jack Sparrow! Or at least someone who looked exactly like Jack Sparrow, with the same outfit, the same dreadlocked hair, and the same swagger. It was as if he were looking in a mirror, although a shadow obscured the impostor's face.

"You've stolen me," the real Jack said angrily, drawing his sword. "And I'm here to take myself back."

The phony Sparrow did the same, and within

seconds Jack found himself in the odd position of having a sword fight with himself. Because, in addition to looking just like him, the impostor fought just like him as well. They matched each other thrust for thrust, lunge for lunge. Even their footwork was identical.

"Stop that!" an annoyed Jack implored.

The sounds of their clashing swords filled the warehouse as they climbed up ramps, over barrels, and under support beams. Through it all, the impostor fought just as Jack would.

"Only one person alive knows that move," Jack pronounced as his alter ego perfectly mimicked one of his most difficult maneuvers.

The next move, however, was one that Jack would never have predicted—the impostor leaned forward and kissed him square on the lips. Suddenly a smile came over Sparrow's face as he recognized it as a kiss he last knew many years ago. The mystery was solved.

"Hello, Angelica," he said as he removed the impostor's hat and fake beard to reveal that the other Jack was actually a beautiful woman.

"Hello, Jack," she replied. "Are you impressed? I think I almost killed you once or twice there."

"I am touched at this most sincere form of flattery," he said. "But why?"

Angelica laughed. "You were the only pirate I thought I could pass for."

Jack thought for a moment. "That is not a compliment," he said.

"Don't worry," she told him. "I have long since forgiven you."

"For leaving you?"

Angelica wagged a finger in his face. "Recall that *I* left you."

Jack shrugged. "A gentleman allows a lady to maintain her fictions."

"And I love this particular fiction," she shot back, proud of her scheme. "First mate Jack Sparrow! As long as my sailors get their money, they will put up with any number of peculiarities."

Jack shook his head. As far as he was concerned,

being impersonated was bad, but being impersonated as a first mate was downright unacceptable. "I
will be impersonated as captain, nothing less," he
declared.

Angelica laughed. "For that you need a ship, and
as it turns out I have one."

Jack nodded. "I could use a ship."

Scrum opened the door and nervously leaned
in. "Milady, I see unseamenlike fellows of the
officious-looking nature." He pointed to the front
of the pub. Jack and Angelica looked out and saw
that the captain of the royal guard and some of his
men were entering. It would not take them long to
make their way back to the warehouse, so Angelica
hurried the conversation along.

"I hear tell you've been to the Fountain," she said.
"The Fountain of Youth."

"There be a lot of hear-telling going on these
days," Jack answered. "Regarding the Fountain—
waste of time, really. Unless you have a few very
specific items of the hard-to-acquire nature."

Before Jack could continue, Scrum opened the door and interrupted. "They're coming."

"Friends of yours?" she asked Jack.

Sparrow smiled. "I may have unintentionally slighted some king or other."

"You have not changed," she said with frustration.

"Implying the need," he responded rakishly.

They could hear the guards getting closer, and Angelica realized that they didn't have much time to resolve their history, so she just got straight to the point.

"You betrayed me. You used me!" she exclaimed. "And what were you doing in a Spanish convent, anyway?"

Jack shrugged. "Honest mistake."

The guards burst into the room, forcing Jack and Angelica to draw their swords and fight side by side. Despite the sword battle, they continued their argument.

"I blame you for this current state of affairs," he said as he blocked one guard's advance. "Your impersonating has caused me a good amount of grief."

Angelica wasn't interested in the present as she still had issues regarding the past. "You ruined my life!" She stopped momentarily to make this point and in the process almost took a sword to the heart, only to be saved by Jack. It quickly became apparent that they could not argue with each other and successfully fight the royal guards. They had to pick sides.

"May I suggest an alliance," she offered as she slashed a rope, which unleashed a stack of barrels that came crashing into the guards. When they hit the floor, the barrels exploded and showered the room with beer.

"Aye," Jack said, agreeing to her offer and trying to drink in a quick sip of the airborne liquor. "Their enemy's enemy is my friend."

Angelica signaled toward the rear of the warehouse. "This way!"

She led him through a maze of crates and barrels until they reached a trapdoor.

"So what is it?" she asked, stopping momentarily.

"What is what?"

"About the Fountain that we need?" she asked, referring to the conversation they were having when the guards interrupted.

According to the legend, some very specific items were necessary to perform the ritual of the Fountain of Youth. "You wouldn't happen to have two chalices. Silver. Once rumored to be in the possession of Ponce de Leon."

She shook her head no and slashed the door open. They could see the Thames River flowing beneath them.

"Desperate disease . . ." she said.

"Requires dangerous remedy," he completed.

They jumped through the opening and came perilously close to the wooden pilings before they splashed down deep into the murky water. Under the surface, they held their breath and started swimming downriver. When they finally came up for air they resumed their argument right where they had left off.

"How could you say I ruined your life?" he asked as they crawled up onto the riverbank.

"You know exactly how!" she said as she gave his face a little push into the mud.

He was about to rebut the charge but then thought better of it. "I do," he admitted.

"Ha!" blurted Angelica, happy to have won something from Jack.

"Oh, and something else," he said.

"You never got over me?" she said flirtingly.

"Regarding the Fountain," he said with a laugh. "There are stories, you know. Rumors that the ritual requires . . ."

"A mermaid," she said. "I know."

Suddenly, Jack felt a sharp pain in his neck. He reached up and plucked out a voodoo dart. His world started spinning, and the last thing he saw was a large man, his eyes completely dead and white, hulking over him.

Just before Jack fainted he uttered one final word: "Zombie."

Chapter Four

THERE WERE FEW PLACES ON EARTH AS terrifying as the execution yard at the Tower of London, where the bodies of long-dead pirates still dangled from the gallows. Burning torches lined the walls, their flickering light casting gruesome shadows across the ground. It was here that Joshamee Gibbs found himself being dragged by two guards. Dragged because he was not about to walk and help them.

"There's been a mistake," he wailed. "It's a life sentence. Not death. Life." His desperate pleas echoed off the stone walls, but there was no one to hear them.

The guards continued to pull him toward the gallows where two white-wigged officials stood waiting to carry out the sentence. Then a ray of hope. He noticed something missing from the gallows.

"You forgot the rope," he said with a laugh. "There's no rope!"

Suddenly Gibbs heard a sound that struck fear even deeper into his heart. It was a boot step followed by a long scrape. Then another boot step followed by another long scrape. This pattern continued and got closer and closer to him until Gibbs could take it no longer. He turned and saw Hector Barbossa, a rope draped over his shoulder.

"Barbossa."

Barbossa signaled the guards. "Off with you." He tossed the rope to Gibbs. "I trust you can tie a noose."

"That's a hard thing," Gibbs protested. "Force a man to twist his own hanging rope."

"You must lie in your bed the way you made

it," Barbossa said coldly. "Where be Jack Sparrow?"

Gibbs couldn't help but smile. If Barbossa didn't know where he was it could only mean one thing. "He escaped?"

Barbossa didn't answer the question, which to Gibbs meant he was right.

"I'm on a tight schedule, Mr. Gibbs," he informed him. "The *Providence* sails at first light and if you do not care to be hanging from a gibbet with a mouth full of flies by then, speak now."

"Take me with you," Gibbs said. "Any point of the compass, a more loyal crewman you won't find."

"Take you where, Mr. Gibbs?" Barbossa asked. "The Fountain? Is that where Jack be headed? Have you anything to offer me? Anything at all?"

Barbossa tossed one end of the rope over the gallows so that the newly tied noose now ominously hung right in front of Gibbs's neck.

"Set me free," Gibbs said. "Then I give you what I have."

Barbossa was still feeling him out, unsure if he

was of any value. "And what might you be having? Upon my naked word you will not see dawn."

Gibbs gulped and pulled a map from his pocket. It was the map Jack had shown him in the paddy wagon. The map he stole in the commotion of their arrival at St. James's Palace.

"Hand it over," Barbossa commanded.

Gibbs would have nothing of it. "You cannot expect I'd be trusting you just like that for nothing."

"In truth," Barbossa said, "I stand before you a man reformed. Reborn. Long since given up me evil ways."

They had sailed together on the *Black Pearl*, and Gibbs had never seen him like this. "A tool of the crown."

"A loyal subject, possessing no will of my own and desiring none, bound by the mandate of my sovereign."

Gibbs was desperate. The only thing worse than Barbossa the pirate was Barbossa the reformed pirate, who'd think nothing of hanging his old crewmate from a gibbet. He knew he had to act quickly if he was to survive. There was a lantern on the gallows, and there Joshamee saw his opportunity. He smashed the lantern on the map, instantly setting it on fire.

Barbossa tried to study it as fast as he could. He could make out a mermaid and two chalices but not the writing next to them. And he saw a dizzying assortment of circles far to complicated to decipher before the flames consumed the map.

"Fool!" he shouted at Gibbs.

Gibbs, though, was no fool. He had just made himself necessary. "I had plenty of time to study those infernal circles and circles within circles," he said of the map. "Every route. Every destination. All safe right here." He tapped his temple to bring the point home. There would be no hanging tonight.

There was only one thing Barbossa could say.

"Welcome back to the navy, Mr. Gibbs."

Chapter Five

THE *Queen Anne's Revenge* WAS ONE OF THE largest, most notorious pirate ships to ever sail the seas. It was just over one hundred feet long, had three tall masts, and carried a crew of more than 125 sailors, including one Jack Sparrow, who was now asleep in a hammock on the main deck. The poison from the voodoo dart had left him unconscious for days, but he was finally stirring.

"Show a leg, sailor," said Scrum, trying to roust him from sleep as quickly as possible so he could begin working.

"Aye, sir!" Jack answered automatically. He rolled out of his hammock and was handed a mop. It took a moment for him to realize what was going on. His last waking vision had been of a white-eyed zombie looming over him. Now he was at sea on a pirate ship, which was troubling enough. But to make matters worse, he was being handed a mop as if he were a lowly deckhand. He was, after all, Captain Jack Sparrow, one of the most infamous pirates of the Caribbean.

"Um, there's been a mistake," he said to Scrum. "I'm not supposed to be here."

Scrum cackled. "Many a man's woken up at sea, no idea what, wherefore, or why, no memory of the night before whence he signed up and drunk away his bonus money."

"No, you see, I am CAPTAIN Jack Sparrow," he said. "The original."

"Scrum," the sailor answered. "The pleasure's all mine. Keep moving."

Scrum forced the mop back into Jack's hand and pushed him to the center of the deck. The officers on the *Revenge* were the most heartless he'd ever encountered. They glared at Scrum and Jack, sending instant shivers down their spines. The two of them couldn't afford to be caught on deck not working.

Jack started mopping while he tried to get his bearings. Suddenly, something unusual caught his eye. He noticed a group of crewmen putting together a narrow box which had sides of glass instead of wood.

"That's a glass coffin," Jack said worriedly to Scrum.

"Aye."

"Why is there a glass coffin?"

Scrum, stopped for a moment. "Do I look like the man in charge?"

"Where am I?" Jack asked one more time.

"Excuse me," Scrum said. "I be right honored to welcome you aboard our eminently infamous vessel, the *Queen Anne's Revenge.*"

Jack knew the name well. And he knew the name of its famous captain, too. "Blackbeard," he said aloud to himself, more than a little worried.

Blackbeard had a murderous reputation. And what Jack saw over the next few hours only confirmed it. Even his flag was intimidating. Most pirates sailed under the Jolly Roger, a black flag sporting a skull and crossbones, but Blackbeard's flag featured the skeleton of the devil sticking a spear into a bloodred heart.

The flag whipped above them as the *Queen Anne's Revenge* raced across the ocean. The ship's sails were full of a hardy wind, and it was accompanied by the sounds of surf against hull and the sight of seagulls flying overhead. Normally, these sounds would have been music to Jack's ears, but he also heard something worrisome. It was the sound of a whip biting into the flesh of deckhands who weren't working hard enough.

The whip was wielded by a quartermaster named Gunner, who stalked the deck and had a terrifying look about him. His lips and one eye were sewn shut.

"That fellow seems odd," Jack mentioned when he passed. "French, is my guess."

Scrum shook his head. "He's been zombie-fied; Blackbeard's doing. All of the officers are that way, keeps them compliant."

Jack nodded. "And perpetually ill-tempered." He flashed a smile at Gunner, who hissed in return.

Something just below the crow's nest caught Jack's attention. The sun was in his eyes so he had to squint, but he could see that a prisoner with his hands tied behind his back was lashed to the mast. The prisoner didn't look like a pirate at all. He had a fresh and wholesome face and wore a frayed cape.

"What did that fellow do?" Jack asked. "And how can I make sure to not?"

"Church fellow, always going on about the Lord Almighty," Scrum explained. "Missionary is the story. What I heard, he got captured in a raid. The rest of the passengers were killed, but not him."

Jack gave him a curious look. It didn't sound like Blackbeard to spare someone during a raid.

"First mate wouldn't let it happen on account of his premier standing with the Lord," he continued. "Odd, if you ask me."

"No," Jack disagreed, looking over his shoulder at Gunner. "*Odd* is standing a-midships back there with a whip."

"A first mate sticking her neck out for some prisoner?" Scrum said. "That you don't see."

Suddenly the picture became much clearer for Jack. "Her?" he asked. "Our first mate is a her?"

Now he at least realized how he had gotten on board. This had to be Angelica's ship and, zombie officers or not, he was determined to confront her. He found her walking along the gun deck. He jumped out to surprise her, holding a sharp cargo hook to her throat.

"You are a ruthless, soulless, cross-grained cur," Jack said.

Angelica smiled. "I told you I had a ship."

"No," Jack corrected. "Blackbeard has a ship. Upon which I am now imprisoned."

Angelica pushed the hook away and looked Jack in the eyes. "We can pull this off, Jack. The Fountain of Youth. Like you always wanted."

Jack gave her a dubious look and motioned in the direction of the captain's quarters.

"Edward Teach," he said, using Blackbeard's real name. "The pirate all pirates fear. Resurrector of the dead in his spare time."

"He'll listen to me," Angelica said.

"He listens to no one," scoffed Jack.

Angelica flashed a devilish smile. "Perhaps his own daughter?"

Apparently, in addition to pretending to be Jack Sparrow in London, she was also pretending to be Blackbeard's daughter. Jack could not believe Angelica would try a scam so daring and dangerous. "Daughter?" he asked. "As in beget by?"

Angelica assumed the same girlish expression she had used on Blackbeard. "Long lost. Recently found. Who loves her dear papa with all her heart and soul."

"Yes, love, but you're not his daughter," Jack expertly pointed out. Angelica then flashed him an evil smile.

"He bought that?" Jack asked, amazed.

Angelica nodded confidently. "I sold that."

Jack considered the situation. "Then it's the Fountain of Youth for him, or him and you. Not you and I."

"No, Jack, that's the best part. He'll be dead."

For years, people had been trying to kill Blackbeard only to wind up dead themselves. Jack had no desire to join them. "You'll be handling that part yourself?" Jack asked.

"There is a prophecy—the man with no eyes," she said, referring to the zombie who had loomed over Jack back in London. "He is known as *eleri ipin*, which means "witness of fate." What he says comes true. He sees things happen before they happen. He's never wrong."

"I can do that, too," Jack mocked. "If you don't count women, weather, and other things that are hard to predict."

CAPTAIN JACK SPARROW wonders
how he got himself into another fine mess.

Rescued from the gallows, **GIBBS** tells Jack about an imposter claiming to be the real Captain Jack Sparrow.

Jack duels against the best swordsman in the Captain's Daughter's pub—himself.

No longer a pirate, privateer **HECTOR BARBOSSA** is now a captain in the king's navy, hunting for the Fountain of Youth—and Captain Jack Sparrow.

THE *QUEEN ANNE'S REVENGE*
is crewed by vicious zombie officers.

Sparks fly as **JACK** and **ANGELICA** are reunited aboard Blackbeard's pirate ship.

Edward Teach, better known as the villainous
BLACKBEARD, is the most notorious
pirate to sail the Seven Seas.

SCRUM gets a kiss from a beautiful-but-deadly mermaid.

Missionary **PHILIP** struggles to help the captured mermaid, **SYRENA**.

The mysterious and beautiful **ANGELICA** is also on
a quest to find the Fountain.

ANGELICA, BLACKBEARD, and **PHILIP** begin the dangerous journey to the fabled Fountain of Youth.

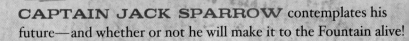

CAPTAIN JACK SPARROW contemplates his future—and whether or not he will make it to the Fountain alive!

Angelica shook her head. "He has seen Blackbeard's death," she replied. "That is a death sentence."

"You believe that?"

Whether or not she believed it wasn't important. "He believes it," she explained. "That's why he needs the Fountain, Jack. He can feel the cold breath of death down his neck."

"Not much to hang your hat on," claimed Jack.

"The prophecy is this," she said with great certainty, "Blackbeard will meet his death within a fortnight at the hands of a one-legged man."

Suddenly Jack's eyes lit up. He happened to know a one-legged man who was also interested in the Fountain of Youth. Maybe this soothsayer *could* see the future.

"Interesting," Jack said, a slight smile forming at the corners of his lips.

Chapter Six

Unlike the *Queen Anne's Revenge* with its zombie officers and motley crew, the HMS *Providence* was sleek, clean, and professional, a proud vessel of the Royal Navy. The three-masted frigate had a long, narrow hull built for speed, making it ideal to charge across the Atlantic in a race to the Fountain of Youth. Meanwhile, the warship's thirty-six cannons meant it was ready should that race turn into a battle. And though he would have probably felt more at home on Blackbeard's ship, Hector Barbossa was pleased to command one belonging to the king.

His last ship had been the *Black Pearl*, and when

she went down he thought he'd never captain a vessel again. Yet here he was striding to the helm. To exude the proper authority, he took shorter steps so his peg leg wouldn't drag. The result was that the tip of the peg made a chilling bang each time it hammered into the wooden deck.

When he took the wheel he paused for a moment, his mind flashing back to the *Pearl* and its fate. It was a brief daydream that one of his officers, Lieutenant Groves, snapped him out of. He cleared his throat and asked, "Orders, sir?"

Barbossa shook off the dark memories of the *Pearl*, relishing the chance to give orders once again. "I'll have my navigator to the helm," he commanded with a crooked-tooth smile.

"Aye, sir," Groves said with a salute before heading belowdecks to retrieve Joshamee Gibbs.

As the ship crashed through the waves and the salt air blew across his face, Barbossa couldn't help but feel two distinct emotions. He was thrilled to be back at sea at the helm of a ship, but he was also concerned about what forces might be awaiting him. For centuries sailing men had tried to locate the Fountain of Youth. And virtually all had met with an untimely fate.

Moments later, Lieutenant Groves returned with Joshamee Gibbs, who by virtue of memorizing the map had become the ship's chief navigator.

"Master Gibbs," Barbossa said, "short we are a map; perhaps ye be so kind as to provide us a heading."

Although he'd been in the navy when he was a much younger man, Gibbs had grown accustomed to the pirate's life, which had far fewer rules and much more beer. He turned to Groves with what he thought was a simple request. "Be a gem and pour me a gulper?"

"Nay," commanded Barbossa. "We be privateers, not pirates, Master Gibbs. And by the gods will behave as such."

"Aye, Captain," Gibbs said with a sigh before adding under his breath, "there is nothing more severe than a reformed anything."

Gibbs looked at the navigation charts and in his mind imagined the dizzying design of circles within circles that he had studied on Jack's map. He turned the map one way and turned his body another. It all had the effect of making Barbossa and his lieutenants wonder if he really knew what he was doing.

"Be we on the proper course, Gibbs?" Barbossa demanded testily.

"Aye, it be proper," Gibbs replied with a nod. "And there's your proof."

He pointed to the horizon, where there were three Spanish galleons with full sails following the same course as the *Providence*.

Barbossa had expected to come into contact with them, but not yet.

"All hands! Battle stations!" he commanded.

The crew raced into action while Barbossa barked out orders, and his second in command, Lieutenant Groves, relayed them to the crew.

"Get to the windward!"

"All hands windward!"

"Harden up two points!"

"Two points!"

"She's built and rigged for hard driving," Barbossa said to Groves with a confident smile. He was determined to put the *Providence* to the test and outrun the Spanish. But the three galleons were fast gaining on him. They were simply much bigger and faster than the *Providence*.

Barbossa prepared to battle. "Cannoneers, take guard position!" he continued. "Silence and await orders."

"Unmoor the guns!" Groves said. "Steady!"

Barbossa was impressed by his crew. They had responded just as ordered and were in proper battle positions. Still, when he looked at the galleons Barbossa realized he stood no chance against the three larger ships. He swore to himself that if another ship went down, he'd be certain to go with it.

He braced for the battle to begin, as did his officers. The crew was frightened but maintained their poise.

Barbossa lifted his spyglass and trained it on the helm of the flagship. There he saw the mysterious dark-skinned man who advised King Ferdinand. A man whom sailors such as Barbossa simply called The Spaniard. His skills were legendary, and everything about him was mysterious.

Much to Barbossa's surprise, The Spaniard wasn't doing anything to prepare for battle. He wasn't even looking at the *Providence*. His eyes were focused on the far horizon, and they stayed that way as the galleons silently sailed past.

"He never even turned his head," Gibbs said in stunned amazement.

"The Fountain is his prize," Barbossa replied. "It appears we're not even worth the time it'd take to sink us. Now we've fallen behind."

Barbossa thought about this for a moment and then screamed. "All hands! Make more sail!"

The crew quickly left their battle stations, determined to make the ship travel as fast as it could.

"RIDE HARD BETWEEN WIND AND TIDE!" Hector bellowed across the ship, that command needing no relay from Groves.

Chapter Seven

WHEN JACK SPARROW CAPTAINED THE *Black Pearl* and Hector Barbossa was his first mate, Barbossa led a mutiny that overtook the ship and left Sparrow to die on a deserted island. So Jack knew a thing or two about mutinies. Now, however, he found himself on the planning side. Angelica may have been confident that she could control Blackbeard, but Jack was not so sure. Add to that an officer corps of zombies, an abused and terrified crew, and Blackbeard's reputation for brutality, and Jack felt it was an entirely unacceptable combination.

He also didn't much care for swabbing the deck.

So he spread word among the crew to meet in a storage cabin on the gun deck of the *Queen Anne's Revenge*.

It was night and the only light was the dim flicker of a candle placed on a wooden crate. This, combined with the ship's creaking, gave the meeting an eerie quality. It was all part of Jack's design to put the crew on edge and make them more likely to join in his scheme. He leaned forward so the candlelight illuminated his face ever so slightly.

"The topic is mutiny," Jack said just above a whisper. "Mutiny most foul."

"Aye," said a crewman named Salaman. "I signed on to sail under Jack Sparrow, not some pretender."

"And a lady at that," added another.

The cook leaned forward. "And mention was failed to be made of this uncanny crew," he said of the zombie officers.

"Curl my toes, they do," added the purser.

Jack knew the best way to incite a crew was to let them incite themselves. He sat back quietly as they continued to list their grievances, and as the list grew, so did their willingness to mutiny. They were still adding to the list when a cabin boy came into the room, his arms loaded with swords he'd taken from the arms cache. "I got them," he said proudly. "All of them." He dumped them onto the crate.

Jack was pleased. He had the crew riled and he had the weapons. All he needed now was to figure out when Blackbeard would be at his most vulnerable. The captain's quarters on the *Revenge* were located in the rear of the ship and were designed to fight a mutiny. With little access in or out, the quarters were well-protected and would be hard for the mutineers to breach. They'd be best to attack when the captain was out on the deck.

"On to it, then," Jack said. "Blackbeard—what are his habits?"

A look passed among the men. Oddly, none seemed to know.

"Stays mostly to his cabin," Scrum offered, while

the others enthusiastically nodded in agreement.

"Yes, but when he comes out?" Jack asked, only to receive blank stares. "He must come out sometime."

Jack looked at the men hopefully, but no one said anything. This seemed suspicious, so he decided to pursue a different line of questioning.

"Any of you sailed with him before?" he asked.

The pirates all looked from one to the other. Surely one of them had sailed with him before, but, again, no one said a word.

Jack couldn't believe what he was hearing. "Stays to his cabin. No one's sailed with him. No one's seen him," Jack said with a laugh. "Good news, gentlemen. This is not Blackbeard's ship. This is not the *Queen Anne's Revenge.*"

The crewmen began to consider this. Was it possible that they had all been duped into believing that this was Blackbeard's ship the same way they had been tricked into believing Angelica was really Jack Sparrow.

"Oh, this is the *Revenge*," Scrum protested.

"How do you know?" asked Jack.

"Seen the name on the side," Scrum said with great certainty.

Jack shook his head. Certainly Scrum wasn't that dumb. Certainly he realized that anyone could have painted a name on the side of a ship. But rather than point out the obvious, he decided to skip ahead. "Gentlemen, a man's first duty is less to his office than to his own honor and that duty we cannot perform if deceived."

"We're decepted then?" asked one of the sailors.

Now it was time for Jack to give them the final push—from being disgruntled to being mutinous. "Aye, you've nay been informed of our destination," he said ominously, using the candlelight effect to its full advantage. "Death lies before us. We sail for the Fountain of Youth."

These men, who had seemed so brave signing up for the pirate's life when they were at the Captain's Daughter, were instantly terrified. Stories had long circulated among sailors about the cursed fate that awaited those who tried to reach the mystical waters of the Fountain. This was not what they had signed on for.

"Death for certain," wailed one.

"The garden of darkened souls!" cried another.

"Untimely our ends will be!"

"Unless," Jack said, seizing the moment, "we take the ship."

Scrum sprang to his feet and grabbed a sword. "We take the ship now!" he said, and he burst out the door to attack.

There was some hesitation among the others, though, and they looked to Jack for confirmation that this was what they were supposed to do.

"We take the ship now!"

On his order the pirates charged through the door and took to the moonlit decks. Each undead officer they encountered was greeted with piercing steel. Then a banshee's wail rang out across the sea.

Jack ran straight for Angelica's cabin. He flung open the door, waking her but not fully. She looked at his silhouette in the doorway. "If this is a dream, you can keep the sword and boots," she said sleepily. "If it's not, you shouldn't be here."

Just then she heard the scream of an officer and the clang of steel clashing with steel. This was real. She jumped from her bed and grabbed her sword.

"We're taking the ship," Jack offered. "Fair warning, you might want . . ."

Before he could even finish, she lunged toward him with her sword. He slammed the door shut just in time, so that the sword pierced it and not his chest.

". . . to stay out of it," he finished from the other side of the doorway.

There was no time for Jack to discuss matters further as he saw the evil Gunner charge toward him. The zombie forced him back, but soon fellow crewmen came to Jack's aid and reversed the charge.

Along with Salaman, Jack climbed the rigging to free Philip the missionary.

"You're either with us or against us!" Salaman exclaimed.

"I am not with you," Philip said. "Neither am I against you."

Salaman didn't know what to make of that and turned to Jack. "Can he do that?"

"He's religious," Jack said. "I believe it's required."

There was no time to debate as the battle still raged. Angelica had now joined the zombies and was fighting valiantly. But the truth was the crew simply outnumbered the officers.

"Fight to the bitter end!" Jack screamed from the rigging, rallying his men. "Take 'em down tight."

Soon after, all of the officers had been subdued. Some were dead and some had been tossed overboard, but most were lashed to the mast.

Jack jumped up on a platform and raised his sword victoriously. "This ship is ours!" he pronounced. To his surprise, this was not greeted by cheers from the men.

Instead, they stared past him with abject terror on their faces. Jack slowly turned around and saw what they did. Silhouetted against the moon was the looming figure of Edward Teach, better known as the notorious Blackbeard.

Chapter Eight

Blackbeard looked across the deck of his ship and tried to control his rage. His officers were lashed to the masts—and his crew had done the lashing.

"Excuse me, gentlemen," he boomed. "I be placed in a bewilderment. I be Edward Teach, Blackbeard, and I be in the captain's quarters. Aye? And that makes me the captain . . . naturally follows."

The crew shuddered with fear, and Jack quickly tried to devise some explanation as Blackbeard walked ominously among them while slowly drawing his sword.

"What of this row on deck," Blackbeard continued. "Sailors abandoned their posts without orders!

Men before the masts taking the ship for their own selves? What be that, first mate?"

"Mutiny!" answered Angelica.

"Aye," Blackbeard said as he continued to walk among them and scrutinize their quivering faces. "And what be the fate of mutineers? We know the answer to that, do we not?" he sneered.

At this point he reached Jack and looked him right in the eye before saying, "Mutineers HANG!"

Without missing a beat, Jack turned on the crew he had so skillfully convinced to mutiny in the first place.

"Captain, sir, I am here to report a mutiny," he offered. "I can name fingers and point names!"

"No need, Mr. Sparrow!" he bellowed. "They are sheep. You, the shepherd."

It seemed as though Blackbeard might run him through right there, but Angelica came to his rescue.

"Father," she reminded him, "he has been . . . to the place where we are going."

Jack happily added, "Have I told you, sir, what a lovely daughter you have?"

"A fitting last sight for a doomed soul," Blackbeard said ominously.

"Mercy, Father," she pleaded. "The seas, the sky, they know nothing of mercy. You can put yourself above them."

Blackbeard thought about this for a moment, then shook his head. "If I don't kill a man every now and then, they forget who I am," he said with a chuckle.

Then an unexpected voice rang out. "Coward!"

All eyes turned to Philip, the missionary, who unlike the others was not scared in the least.

"They do not forget," he said. "Your crew see you for the miscreant you are. A coward no matter how many you slay."

Blackbeard could not believe anyone would speak to him in such a manner. On his own ship no less. "Twice in one day, I find myself in a bewilderment," he wailed.

Philip did not back down. "You are not bewildered. You are afraid. You dare not walk the path of righteousness, the way of the light."

"No, sir. The fact of it be much simpler than all that," he said as he leaned in close to the missionary. "I am a bad man."

He gave the command to kill Philip, but once again Angelica came to the rescue.

"No, Father, you must not!" she said as she drew her sword and stood between them.

"I am again forgetting my daughter fears for my soul," he said. "Endless damnation, the fiery pit, should I strike down an emissary of the Lord. Worse than all my other sins put together. Is that the way of it?"

Angelica nodded.

He looked at her and wondered. At times she was as wily and able a pirate as he'd ever known. But she was also the God-fearing girl who'd been raised in a convent.

"You truly hope to save me?" he asked her softly.

"Every soul can be saved," she answered with conviction.

Blackbeard looked to the missionary. "Be that true, young cleric?"

Philip nodded. "Yes, though you I see as a bit of a long shot. Still, I pray for every unfortunate soul on this hell-bound vessel."

"You disarm me with your faith," Blackbeard replied before turning back to the others. Still, there'd been an attempted mutiny and someone had to pay.

"Which wretched soul stood watch?" he called out.

It was certain that whoever was on watch would pay the price for the mutiny. And, even though it was not him, Jack stepped forward.

"Me," he said. "I stood watch, sir."

Blackbeard laughed and shook his head. He knew it was not Sparrow. The pirate turned to the zombie Gunner, who nodded in the direction of the ship's cook.

"Aye, the cook," Blackbeard said. "Perfect. Lower the longboat."

A few moments later, a longboat was lowered from the *Queen Anne's Revenge*. Its only passenger was the cook, the lone crew member Blackbeard had decided to punish as an example for those who had mutinied.

The longboat bobbed up and down on the large ocean waves, and the cook began to row as fast as he could. He didn't stand much of a chance against the pirate ship, but he was going to give it his best effort.

"Bring her about!" Blackbeard commanded to his zombie officers, who resumed their positions in control of the ship. They began turning the *Queen Anne's Revenge* so that it would face the cook's boat.

"Mercy, Father," pleaded Angelica.

"Mutiny, Daughter," he replied coldly. "Our laws be clear."

"'Blessed are the merciful, for they will receive mercy,'" she said, quoting a Bible verse she learned in the convent.

"It is a blessing for a man to have a hand in determining his own fate," Blackbeard responded. "A gift not afforded to all of us."

In truth, the cook had little hand in his fate. No matter how hard he rowed, he couldn't escape the evil Blackbeard had planned for him.

"Course made!" Blackbeard barked once the ship had lined up with the longboat.

"Stop," pleaded Philip. "Give that man a chance."

It was too late. A terrifying flame shot forward from the mouth of the skeleton-shaped figure at the front of the ship. It was unlike anything Jack had ever seen—fire that burned on water. Fire that seemed supernatural.

The cook screamed in agony when the flames reached his boat. A wild-eyed Blackbeard turned to Philip. "Perhaps you will pray for him to be unharmed?" he said with a sneer.

"Please," Philip yelled over the screams of the cook. "There is still hope for that man."

"Again," Blackbeard commanded, ignoring the missionary.

One of the zombie officers wore a menacing smile as he lit the fuse and unleashed another burst of flame out across the water.

The screams continued for a few more terrifying

moments. Then all went silent except for the sound of the tide washing against the boat.

After this display, Blackbeard knew he would not face another mutiny from his crew. But he still had to deal with Sparrow, the man he'd rightly identified as the leader of the revolt. He had the quartermaster drag Jack to his cabin and throw him down hard against the bulkhead.

Blackbeard loomed over him for a moment, causing Jack to doubt that his place among the living was secure.

"I've no interest in the Fountain," Jack said. "So if your heart's set, just drop me off anywhere."

"Your words surround you like fog," Blackbeard said. "Make you hard to see."

"What of you, the mighty Blackbeard?" Jack said. "Here you are, running scared."

"Scared?" asked Blackbeard.

"To the Fountain."

"Every soul has an appointment with death. In my case I happen to know the exact time,"

Blackbeard replied with a smile. "I must reach the Fountain. It be foolish to battle fate, but I am pleased to cheat it."

Just then Angelica came into the cabin.

"Oh, good. He's still alive," she said, seeing Jack healthy and breathing. "You will lead us to the Fountain? Yes?"

Jack squirmed for a moment, and Blackbeard leaned in closer. "Put another way," Blackbeard said, "if I don't make it there in time . . . neither will you."

Just then there was a surprise arrival at the door. It was the quartermaster with the cook. The same cook who'd been fired on. He wasn't dead. But he wasn't exactly alive either. The fire was part of a voo-doo ritual that had transformed him. He was now a zombie, just like the other officers on the ship. Jack looked into his cold dead eyes and knew his was a fate worse than death. He also realized that he could be next and made a decision on the spot.

"I'll have a look-see at those charts, straight-away," he said cheerily. "If you don't mind?"

Chapter Nine

WITH A SLIGHT SPRAY OF OCEAN MIST IN his face and a strong wind filling his ship's sails, Hector Barbossa was enjoying his return to the seafaring life. The HMS *Providence* was slashing through the waves on a course for the Spanish Main, which is what sailors called the mainland areas that surrounded the Caribbean Sea. There had been no more sightings of the galleons or pirate ships. And unlike Blackbeard aboard the *Queen Anne's Revenge*, Barbossa didn't have a disgruntled crew to deal with.

Or so he thought.

As he sat back and relaxed, eating slices of

apple from a fine silver plate, Lieutenant Groves approached with a few members of the crew behind him.

"Aye?" Barbossa asked as he bit into a crisp slice.

"Captain, sir," Groves stammered, "I am unhappy to report rumors, sir, among the crew as to our destination."

Barbossa didn't want to hear a thing about it. "Shut yer traps and make way," he barked. But Groves and the men did not move.

"No disrespect, sir," Groves said.

Barbossa sighed. "What do the men fear?"

"Whitecap Bay."

Barbossa expected as much. "Every worthless seaman fears the name, rightly so, though few know why or dare to ask."

Joshamee Gibbs looked up from a navigational chart. "Be the stories true?" he asked, unwilling to even say the word that scared him.

"Listen that your voice should quiver like a

fiddle string!" admonished Barbossa. "Say what robs you of your staunch heart, Gibbs, or forever leave it to the wide fields of fancy."

Gibbs cleared his throat. "Mermaids, sir."

"Aye, mermaids," Barbossa said with a nod. "Sea ghouls, devil fish, dreadful in hunger for the flesh of man. Mermaid waters—that be our path."

Murmurs of fear spread through the assembled members of the crew.

"Cling to your soul, Mister Gibbs, as mermaids be given to take the rest, to the bone," continued Barbossa.

"Steady men, find your courage," Groves commanded. "Or be ready to purpose your fear."

For one of the sailors, the thought of coming face-to-face with a deadly mermaid was simply too much to bear. He sprinted to the side of the ship, dived into the ocean, and started swimming to a far-off island on the horizon.

"Man overboard!" Groves yelled.

"Nay," corrected Barbossa. "A deserter."

Groves couldn't believe it. "Come about, sir?"

"Nay," Barbossa said as he started to address the crew directly, hoping to boost their resolve. "I shan't ask any more of a man than what that man can deliver. But I do ask, are we not King's men?"

The crewmen straightened upright. A few even answered: "Aye."

"On the king's mission?" he continued. "I did not note any fear in the eyes of the Spanish as they passed us by."

Now the crew was embarrassed.

"Are we not King's men?" Barbossa asked more forcefully.

"Aye" was the response, this time given much more enthusiastically.

"Aye," agreed Barbossa as he barked out a new set of orders. "Double-reef the mizzen topsail and hoist it up! Haul her close! Stave on ahead!" the navy captain commanded.

The crew members scurried into their positions, ready to take on whatever dangers they might face.

Joshamee Gibbs, though, was apprehensive as he watched the deserter swimming toward the faraway island and wondered if he had the right idea.

"And may God have mercy on our souls."

Chapter Ten

ON A MOONLESS NIGHT, SEVERAL LONGBOATS made their way from the *Queen Anne's Revenge* toward an ancient pier on Whitecap Bay. None of the passengers said a word. The only sounds were of the oars slapping against the water and the surf crashing into the rocky coast.

When they tied up to the pier, some of the pirates began dragging large, thick nets onto the dock.

"Lay 'em out flat, no tangles," commanded Blackbeard as he walked amongst them. "Mend the holes. Make 'em look purty for our dainty guests!" he added with a frightening chuckle.

Blackbeard turned to the members of his landing

party, which included Jack, Angelica, and Salaman. "We're going to need a light," he said. "A lot of light."

He motioned to an abandoned lighthouse on the point, and while the rest of the pirates went about preparing the nets, Jack and the others headed for it.

As they climbed the wooden steps that led to the top, Jack tried to explain to a young sailor what they were up against as well as the details of the ritual that was to be performed at the Fountain.

"We require a mermaid's tear. So, we require a mermaid," he said.

"So?" asked the sailor.

Jack stopped for a moment and gave the young man a look. "You ever seen a mermaid? You start with a shark. Give them weapons. And make them all women."

"Beautiful women?"

"Did you miss the part about the sharks?" Jack asked, shaking his head.

"I heard Jack Sparrow once had the favor of mermaids," the sailor answered.

Jack couldn't help but flash a little gold-toothed smile. "Is that story still out there? A mermaid's favor, perhaps," Jack continued. "That I might believe."

"Is there a female anywhere, of any kind, safe from you?" asked Angelica.

Finally they reached the upper level of the lighthouse tower. The door had long since rotted and was off its hinges. The actual light mechanism was complex and well-weathered. It had a rotating platform, a large mirror, and a system of pipes leading back to a very large tank.

All eyes turned to Salaman, who was most experienced with this type of equipment. It had fallen on him to get it running.

"Smell that?" he asked. "Whale oil. Stuff burns like a miracle from God."

"Can you make it work?" asked Blackbeard, pointing to the mechanism.

Salaman, who was Indian, didn't think much of the design. "Made by the English," he scoffed. "Let's not get our hopes up." As he went to work on the equipment, Jack stepped to the edge of the platform to take in the view of the bay. Angelica stepped up behind him.

"The old moon in the new moon's arms," she said. "First of the summer. Perfect for a mermaid hunt."

"How so?" asked Jack.

"Mating season," she said with a shark's smile.

Jack shook his head. He was not at all envious of what some of his crewmates were about to encounter.

Down below on the water was another longboat with a specially selected crew of inexperienced sailors, who were easy to replace should they not survive. Keeping them in line was the zombie quartermaster, Gunner, ready to draw his pistol.

"We're doomed," said a pirate named Ezekiel.

"We're not doomed," offered another named Derrick. "Day we set sail, I spilled a glass of wine on deck. That's good luck," he said, hoping it was true.

Scrum countered with, "But when the clothes of

a dead sailor are worn by another sailor during the same voyage, misfortune will befall the entire crew!"

The rest of the men looked at him in shock and disbelief. "I'm just sayin'" he quickly replied.

Just then, the beam from the lighthouse came to life. It panned across the water until it found the men and then it held firm.

"They be drawn to man-made light," Derrick offered.

"Sharks?" asked the cabin boy.

"Worse than sharks," answered Ezekiel. "There'll be mermaids upon us within the hour. Mark my words, sharks won't dare come near."

Derrick smiled, his crooked yellow teeth visible in the light beam. "I hear it said a kiss from a mermaid protects a sailor from drowning. And sometimes the song of a mermaid will lead a ship away from the shoals."

"Don't be a fool," scolded Ezekiel. "Mermaids are all female and lovely as a dream of heaven. But they snatch a sailor out of a boat or off of the deck of a ship, and the sailors are pulled to the bottom and drowned or eaten."

With this story, the mood on the longboat took a turn for the worse. The pirates desperately tried to come up with a way to get out of their situation when Gunner pointed his pistol at Scrum.

"Sing."

"What?" asked Scrum.

Gunner explained, "They like to hear singing."

Although Scrum was good with a mandolin, he wasn't a particularly skilled singer. Worse, the only song he knew well was a sea chantey written for a girl.

"*My name it is Maria, a merchant's daughter fair,*" he mumbled with little sense of musicality.

"Louder!" demanded Gunner.

"*And I have left my parents and three thousand pounds a year.*"

While Scrum's awful singing carried across the water, other longboats moved silently through the darkness. They carried large barrels and silent crews.

Gunner motioned to the other pirates with his pistol, which was all the convincing they needed to join in the singing.

"*My heart is pierced by Cupid, I disdain all glittering gold,*" they sang. "*There is nothing can console me but my jolly sailor bold.*"

Just then Philip, the missionary, spotted a ripple on the water. He pointed at it, and the others looked to see a smiling, luminescent mermaid break the surface at the bow of the boat. She was lovely, with golden hair and pale skin. She swam alongside the boat and resurfaced next to Scrum. She was the most beautiful creature any of them had ever seen.

"Do you talk?" asked Scrum, mesmerized.

"Yes," she answered with a giggle. "Are you the one who sings?"

Scrum flashed a proud smile. "Aye."

The mermaid smiled radiantly. "Are you 'my jolly sailor bold'?" she asked, repeating the line from the song.

"Aye, that I be," he said, leaning over the edge of the boat toward the mermaid.

"Scrum—comport yourself," warned Philip as he and the other pirates pulled him back toward the middle of the boat.

"Boys, there ain't much been given me in my brief miserable life," he said, breaking free and moving back toward the edge. "But by God I'll have it said, Scrum had himself a kiss from a mermaid!"

The mermaid smiled and began singing. "*My heart is pierced by Cupid, I disdain all glittering gold.*"

Suddenly a host of mermaids surrounded the boat, each one luring a different pirate.

The first mermaid continued singing, "*There's nothing can console me but my jolly sailor bold.*"

Just as she finished the line, Scrum leaned over for a kiss, and the mermaid rose closer to him, but as she did, she unleashed a bloodcurdling shriek, and the kiss became a bite as she pulled him under the surface.

Without warning, the other mermaids attacked

and pulled the remaining pirates into the ocean. A feeding frenzy broke out as mermaids appeared everywhere and pirates screamed into the darkness.

Suddenly the pirates on the other longboats sprang into action.

"Harden up!" the purser called across the boats. Muster your courage!"

The men lit the fuses on their barrels, which were filled with gunpowder, and dropped them into the water. KABOOM! In seconds, the barrels started to explode, sending columns of water climbing to the sky. KABOOM!

The shrieks of the mermaids turned into wails of pain.

Now fire started shooting out from the mouth of the skeleton on the front of the *Queen Anne's Revenge*, the flames dancing along the water's surface.

Back in the lighthouse, the pirates watched in horror as the battle unfolded.

"Out upon it," Blackbeard commanded as his

torch burned along the waterline. "It's begun!"

Crewmen bravely waded into the water, ready to toss their heavy nets over any mermaid that got close.

"A gold doubloon to the man who spots the first!" Blackbeard called out as he rushed along the pier. "Do not be greedy! We need but a single one!"

When the explosions stopped, there was an eerie calm. All the mermaids had disappeared beneath the surface. As he walked among the pirates, Jack got more and more nervous. He had faced these deadly creatures before and knew what they were capable of. Suddenly, one of the pirates was sucked beneath the surface, barely able to gasp before he disappeared into the dark waters. Then another. The mermaids were attacking from below.

"Retreat, all!" Jack called out as he ran through the shallow water toward land. "For your lives!"

The pirates charged toward the shore, but Blackbeard was there waiting for them, his torch in hand as he yelled at them. "Back in the water!

Cowards! There be no refuge on land, on my word!"

Jack was more scared of the mermaids than he was of Blackbeard. He continued his retreat to the beach as mermaid hands reached up from the water and grabbed at his feet and ankles.

When he reached the beach, he realized that he was one of the only ones to have made it to safety. Behind him, the bay was filled with mermaids battling against overmatched pirates. The screams and cries blended together so that it was impossible to distinguish one being from another.

But it was obvious that the mermaids would win. Blackbeard's quest to cheat death had endangered every man in his crew. And while Jack was not normally heroic, he cared about his shipmates and wanted to help them. He needed a weapon to swing the battle in the pirates' favor. That's when he remembered the lighthouse.

At the top of it was a large tank filled with whale oil. It was oil that Salaman said burned "like a miracle from God." Jack wondered if he might be able to make a miracle out of it.

He raced up the wooden steps to the top of the lighthouse. The flame was burning as it was supposed to, just a little bit at a time, enough to illuminate the lighthouse. Jack took out his sword and slammed it into the valve so that the oil began spraying out in every direction, coating the entire light room.

The oil actually came out faster than he had expected, so Jack jumped through the window just as it reached the flame. The entire top of the lighthouse exploded into one giant fireball. It rocked the entire beach and blasted across its surface.

The mermaids shrieked in terror and momentarily let go of their victims. That was just the break the pirates needed as they rushed toward the beach and safety.

Jack crashed to the ground as the explosions continued. "Did everyone see that, because I will not be doing it again," he said. And he didn't have to. The mermaids had retreated and that the pirates were swimming for freedom. He had saved the day.

"Check the wounded and see if any can be saved," Blackbeard commanded as he walked along the destruction on the beach.

A pirate went to help a wounded crewmate and Blackbeard scolded him.

"Not us, them!" he commanded. "Find one still alive!"

There among the debris they saw a mermaid, injured but still alive. She was trapped in a tidal pool and unable to swim to freedom.

"We got one!" yelled Blackbeard with a cackle as some pirates began to wrap her tightly in a net.

The pirates loaded the very beautiful but very deadly mermaid, named Syrena, into a water-filled coffin for her journey to the Fountain. She was now a part of this motley crew and their strange voyage—whether she liked it or not. And she most assuredly did not.

Chapter Eleven

THE *Queen Anne's Revenge* HAD LOWERED ITS three-thousand-pound anchors into the still waters of a hidden cove, safe from the Spanish, the British, and perhaps most importantly, the mermaids.

Now the pirates had moved onto a beach of hard-packed sand surrounded by dense jungle. Four men carried the glass coffin that had worried Jack when he first awoke on the *Revenge*. Only now he realized it wasn't a coffin. It was a human-size aquarium half-filled with water and holding a mermaid.

Blackbeard walked up to Jack and flashed a menacing look.

"It's up to you now, Sparrow," he said, the implication being that failure was not an option.

Jack shrugged and pulled out his compass. Unlike most compasses, which always pointed north, Jack's always pointed in the direction of what he wanted most. It was somewhat mystical.

"What I want first," Jack decreed, "is Ponce de Leon's ship."

The needle on Jack's compass began to tremble and then it turned until it faced in a new direction. Jack smiled and slapped it shut. He told the others to follow, and they began their trek into the jungle.

After half a day of walking, everyone was getting hot and tired. One of the men carrying the aquarium was Scrum, who was scratched and bruised but lucky to have survived his encounter with the mermaid. He wasn't thrilled that they were bringing this one along with them.

"Why is it we got to bring her along?" he asked.

"Tears don't keep," Angelica explained. "We need them fresh."

Angelica walked up alongside Jack, who was leading the way.

"Now what is that ritual again?" he asked. "Water from the Fountain and a mermaid's tear . . ."

"And two silver chalices," Angelica continued. "One cup with the tear and one without."

"So one with a tear? And water in both?" Jack asked, getting a bit confused. "These things can get complicated."

"I'm going to say it again," Angelica replied, her frustration level rising. "Both get water. One gets a tear. The person who drinks the water with the tear gets all the years of life from the other."

Jack scratched his head. "Run it by me again? Slowly? You need two chalices?"

Frustrated, Angelica started cursing in Spanish.

In truth, Jack knew the legend well. And he knew that they could not do a thing without the silver chalices from Ponce de Leon's ship.

He continued in the same direction until he reached a tall chasm that overlooked a rocky river. The remains of an ancient bridge were there, but it had long since been destroyed. There was no way to cross to the other side.

"As I thought," Jack announced. "Not this way."

Angelica didn't believe him. His compass was always right. "This is the way, isn't it?"

"We can go around to the east," Jack offered.

Angelica shook her head. "But that takes us out of the path of the chalices?"

Jack didn't want to admit she was right, so he offered an alternative. "Well, then we circle back."

"We don't have the time," she implored.

"Well, you insisted on bringing a mermaid," Jack offered.

She gave him a look. "The mutiny didn't help."

Blackbeard stepped between them to stop the bickering and state the obvious.

"Someone must go," he said, pointing at the chasm.

"You mean, jump?" Jack asked. "This I cannot wait to see."

Blackbeard looked him square in the eye. "You will go," he told Jack. "Find the ship and retrieve the chalices."

"Jack?" Angelica protested. "What makes you think he will come back?"

Jack nodded in agreement and repeated it. "'What makes you think he will come back?'"

"We cannot trust him," Angelica said. "I'll go."

"She'll go," Jack said with a smile.

Blackbeard shook his head. "How much farther to the Fountain?"

"A day's march north," Jack answered honestly. "Follow that river until you reach a series of pools. Then you're close."

Blackbeard took the compass from Sparrow's hand. "Jack will go," he announced.

Jack shook his head. "You know the feeling you get, sometimes, standing in a high place? A sudden urge to jump? I'm not feeling that."

Blackbeard pulled his pistol and trained it on Jack's head.

"I need those chalices!" Blackbeard demanded.

"Shoot," Jack said. "It will save me the trouble of the fall."

Blackbeard thought about this for a moment and turned so that the pistol was now pointed at Angelica. A look of worry passed over Jack's face.

"You will go and you will return," the evil pirate said. "Or I will kill her."

Jack looked at Angelica and the very real fear on her face. He had no doubt that Blackbeard would kill his own daughter. And he had no doubt that he would kill Jack next. He weighed the options in his head, but no matter how he arranged them he didn't like the results.

Captain Jack Sparrow was a lot of things, but courageous was not the most obvious. Perhaps this act wasn't truly courageous. Perhaps he just did the math and realized his best chance was to take a leap of faith.

With a deep breath, Jack ran with all his strength and jumped from the edge of the chasm, screaming like a frightened baby the whole way down—until his body slammed into the river.

Miraculously, he came back to the surface, still breathing. He could not believe that he was still alive, but he was.

"Wet again," he said aloud to himself with a chuckle as he scrambled toward the riverbank.

Jack continued in the direction his compass had laid out. It took him down the river, through the jungle, and after a few hours of hiking to a cliff-side beach. There, perched upon the cliff, were the wrecked remains of a square-masted Spanish sailing vessel.

Jack knew it the second he saw it.

"The *Santiago*," he said aloud as though someone were with him. "Famously captained by Ponce de Leon."

Jack flashed the smile that had gotten him into and out of so much trouble. He still had to retrieve the chalices and make it to the Fountain, but to Jack Sparrow these were just minor obstacles. The legend of the Fountain of Youth was a legend no more. It was now real. The ship was real, and the chalices were on board. Blackbeard and his men had captured a mermaid and were taking her to the Fountain. That meant Jack would have everything he needed to perform the ritual and unleash the power of the Fountain.

But that wasn't the only thing on Jack's mind. He had more motivation than just eternal life. There was Angelica, perhaps the only woman he had ever loved. Years before, he had abandoned her and broken her heart. Now he had a chance to save her from the evil Blackbeard. And then there was Blackbeard himself, a bloodthirsty pirate who had endangered everybody for his own benefit. Surely Jack had to do something about him, even if it cost him his very life.

"Dead men tell no tales."

That was the warning pirates offered those

who braved the seas. But once again, Captain Jack Sparrow had shown it wasn't necessarily true. He'd been chased by a king, condemned to hang, shanghaied aboard Blackbeard's ship, tossed in a sea of mermaids, and had even jumped from a cliff that no man could survive.

Yet here he was, poised for the greatest adventure of all. He was prepared to face down the nefarious Blackbeard in an attempt to rescue the beautiful Angelica and drink from the famed Fountain of Youth. If a dead man could tell such tales, imagine the stories that could be told by a man who drank from those immortal waters.

The smile only got bigger as he thought about the endless possibilities. The horizon was calling, and Captain Jack Sparrow was ready to answer, even if it meant having to sail on stranger tides. . . .

BEFORE THE *BLACK PEARL*,
THERE WAS A TEENAGE
STOWAWAY NAMED
JACK SPARROW . . .

Before he sailed on stranger tides and
was at the world's end, before he was after the Dead
Man's Chest, and even before he was known as Captain
Jack Sparrow—he was simply known as Jack, a teenage
pirate who sailed on the *Barnacle* with a ragtag crew,
unharmed by ancient curses. Yet Jack always had a
desire for adventure. This time, Jack and his young crew
are on a quest for the legendary Sword of Cortés, which
possesses unimaginable powers. But can Jack survive
against dangerous pirates, like the notorious Captain
Torrents and Left-Foot Louis, who are after the same
treasure? And can he and his crew remain safe from the
dark, eerie spells of the mysterious creatures that line
the ocean floor? Be here to find out, and to discover
how Young Jack becomes the infamous Captain Jack
Sparrow . . . and especially how he got that dashing hat.

Chapter One

A DIM MOON ROSE OVER THE OCEAN AS THE wind blew thickening clouds across the sky. Faint shadows were cast upon the island below: huge, black sailing ships, sea monsters, and other things that haunted the midnight waters seemed to cascade over the hills. Few stars were strong enough to twinkle through the stormy haze. The white sands of the beach were swept into little whirlwinds, shifting the patterns on the sand dunes.

A bad night for sailing.

The few respectable citizens of Tortuga stayed snug in their well-guarded houses. Everyone else— buccaneers, swashbucklers, and cutthroats all—was down at the Faithful Bride, drinking ale and rum.

Between gusts of wind from the gathering storm, the noise from the tavern could be heard a half mile away. Laughing, shouting, and the occasional burst of gunfire echoed through the night as drinkers took up a chanty they all knew:

> Yo ho, yo ho, a pirate's life for me!
> We kindle and char and inflame and ignite—
>   drink up me hearties, yo ho!
> We burn up the city, we're really a fright—
>   drink up me hearties, yo ho!
> Yo ho, yo ho, a pirate's life for me . . .

From outside, the Faithful Bride looked like nothing more than an oversize shack. It wasn't even built out of proper wood, but from the timbers of wrecked boats. It smelled like a boat, too: tar and salt and seaweed and fish. When a light rain finally began to fall, the roof leaked in a dozen places.

Inside, no one seemed to care about the puddles on the floor. Tankards were clashed together for toasts, clapped on the table for refills, and occasionally thrown at someone's head.

It was crowded this night, every last shoddy chair filled in the candle-lit tavern. I reckon we have enough old salts here to crew every ship in Port Royal, the Faithful Bride's young barmaid, Arabella, thought. She was clearing empty mugs off a table surrounded by men who were all hooting at a story. Like everyone in the pub, they were dressed in tattered, mismatched garb common to all the "sailors" of the area: ragged breeches, faded waistcoats, stubbly beards, and the odd sash or belt.

One of them tugged on her skirt, grinning toothlessly.

Arabella rolled her eyes and sighed. "Let me guess," she said, tossing aside her tangled auburn locks. "Ale, ale, ale and . . . oh, probably another ale?"

The sailor howled with laughter. "That's my lass!"

Arabella took a deep breath and moved on to the other tables.

"There's no Spanish treasure left but inland, ye daft sprog," a sailor swore.

"I'm not talkin' about Spanish treasure," his friend, the second-rate pirate Handsome Todd said, lowering his voice. There was a gleam in his eye, not yet dulled by drink. "I'm talkin' about Aztec Gold, from a whole lost kingdom...."

Arabella paused and listened in, pretending to pick a mug up off the floor.

"Yer not talking about Stone-Eyed Sam and Isla Esquelética?" the sailor replied, skeptically. "Legend says Sam 'e had the Sword of Cortés, and 'e cursed the whole island. Aye, I agree with only one part of that story—that it's legend. Legend, mate. 'A neat little city of stone and marble—just like them there Romans built,' they say. Bah! Rubbish! Aren't nothing like that in the Caribbean, I can tell you!"

"Forget the blasted kingdom and the sword, it's his gold I'm talking about," Handsome Todd spat out. "And I can tell you, I know it's real. Seen it with my own eyes, I have. It changes hands often, like it's got legs all its own. But there are ways of finding it."

"Ye got a ship, then?" the first sailor said with a leery look in his eyes.

"Aye, a fine little boat, perfect for slipping in and out of port unseen . . ." Handsome Todd began. But then he noticed Arabella, who was pretending to wipe something from the floor with her apron. She looked up and gave him a weak smile.

She looked again at the floor and rubbed fiercely with the edge of her apron. "Blasted men, spillin' their ale," she said.

Handsome Todd relaxed. But he looked around suspiciously as if the other buccaneers, the walls, or the King himself were listening. "Let's go somewhere a bit quieter, then, shall we? As they say, dead men tell no tales."

Arabella cursed and moved away. Usually, no one cared—no one noticed if she were there or not. To the patrons of the Bride, she was just the girl who filled the tankards. She had heard hundreds of stories and legends over the years.

Each story was almost like being on an adventure.

Almost.

Still, she decided, not a bad night, considering. It could have been far worse. A storm often seemed to bring out the worst in an already bad lot of men.

And then, suddenly, the door blew open with gale force.

A crash of lightning illuminated the person in the doorway. It was a stranger, wet to the bone. Shaggy black hair was plastered against his head, and the lightning glinted in his eyes. Arabella held her breath—she had never seen anyone like him before.

Then the door slammed shut, and the candlelight revealed an angry, dripping, young man—no older than Arabella. There was silence for a moment. Then the patrons shrugged and returned to their drinks.

The stranger began to make his way through the crowd, eyes darting left and right, up and down like a crow's. He was obviously looking for someone, or something. His jaw was set in anger.

His hazel eyes lit up for a moment: he must have found what he was looking for. He bent down behind a chair, and reached for something. Arabella stood on her tiptoes to see—it just looked like an old sack. Not at all worth stealing from the infamous pirate who was guarding it.

"Oh, no . . ." Arabella whispered.

The stranger bit his lip in concentration. He stretched his fingers as long and narrow as possible, discreetly trying to reach between the legs of the chair.

Without warning—and without taking the drink from his lips—the man who sat in the chair rose up, all seven feet and several hundred pounds of him. His eyes were the color of a storm, and they sparked with anger.

The stranger pressed his palms together and gave a quick bow.

"Begging your pardon, Sir, just admiring my . . . I mean your fine satchel there," he said, extremely politely.

The pirate roared and brought his heavy tankard down, aiming for the stranger's head.

The stranger grabbed the sack and sidestepped just in time. The mug whistled past his ear . . .

. . . and hit another pirate behind him!

This other pirate wasn't as big, but he was just as irritable. And armed. And he thought the stranger was the one who had just hit him in the head with a tankard! The pirate drew a rapier and lunged for the stranger.

The stranger scooted backward, moving out of the way of the deadly blade. His second attacker kept going, falling forward into the table where the giant pirate had been sitting. The rickety table broke under his weight, and drinks, coins, and knives flew into the air. The buccaneers around the table leapt up, drawing their swords and pistols.

It didn't take much to start a barroom brawl in Tortuga.

The Faithful Bride exploded with the sounds of punches, groans, screams, yells and hollers, the clash of cutlasses striking rapiers, and the snap of wood as chairs were broken over heads. All this, in addition to the sound of the crashing thunder and the leaking ceiling that began to pour down on the brawling patrons.

The stranger was caught in the middle of it. And to make matters worse, the giant pirate was still after him.

The huge pirate drew his sword and swung it at the stranger. The stranger leapt up onto the chair behind him, the blade slicing the air where he had just stood.

"That's a bit close, mate," the stranger said. He jumped off the chair again and kicked at one of its legs, causing it to flip up into the air and land in his hands.

The giant swung again, but the stranger held the chair like a shield, blocking every strike. Bits of wood flew off the chair where the blade hit.

Another pirate dove for the stranger—or maybe for someone behind him, it was hard to tell at this point. The stranger leaned out of the way, just barely avoiding the collision, and his attacker toppled into the giant pirate.

With the giant now otherwise engaged, the stranger hoisted the sack onto his shoulder, turned around and surveyed the scene behind him. What was—for pirates—a fairly quiet night of drinking, had turned into yet another bloody and violent brawl like the others he'd seen in his day. He couldn't resist grinning.

"Huh. Not a single bruise on me," he said out loud. "Not one blasted scratch on Jack Sparrow."

Then someone smashed a bottle against a timber above his head. The giant had risen behind him, surprisingly quiet for such a large man. Jack swung around to see him and began to back away.

"You'll just be giving me that sack now, boy," the pirate said in a deadly voice, holding the broken bottle before him and pointing it at Jack.

"Uh . . ." Jack looked around, but he was surrounded by the fight on all sides, still blocked from the door.

"Good Sir . . ." he began, hoping something would come to him. But before he could think of a way out of this one, the giant roared and bolted forward.

A hand grabbed Jack by the collar and yanked him out of the way. But it happened so quickly that the giant kept running and crashed right into a group of a half-dozen pirates who were battering each other along the far wall. There was a crack of wood, a crash of glass, and a blast of rolling thunder from the storm outside. The angry pirates all turned toward the not-so-gentle giant and pounced on him.

Arabella kept a very firm grip on Jack's collar as she pulled him quickly through the crowd, ducking and avoiding the brawling sailors. And Jack kept a very firm grip on the sack. His sack.

After a few more near misses, Jack and Arabella staggered out the back door and into the stormy tropical night.

Chapter Two

It WAS RAINING MUCH HARDER NOW, AND THE wind had picked up incredible speed. Jack and the barmaid were in an alley behind the tavern, and the slight overhang wasn't keeping them dry. He turned to thank the girl who had saved him, but before he could, she threw him up against the side of the Faithful Bride.

"How dare ye start a fight in my father's tavern?" She placed her hands on her hips and her brown eyes flashed. "Couldn't ye do your pickpocketing somewhere else tonight? Someplace nicer, whose patrons wouldn't wreck the place?" She pushed him against the wall and stepped back.

Jack brushed himself off, straightening the

wrinkles in his coat. "Now listen here, lassie, I am not a thief. I didn't come here by choice. And I wasn't pickpocketing." Jack waved the sack in Arabella's face. "Captain 7-foot-beastie in there stole my sack here, and I was simply reclaiming my property. So if my gratitude is worthless to you, I'll just gather up my things, not say 'thank you' for being so inhospitable, and be on my merry way. Savvy?"

Jack lifted his head up and started to walk. But Arabella grabbed his arm and threw him up against the wall again.

"Do you have any idea who you've taken that sack from—whether it's yours or not?" she asked.

"No. And truth be told, I do not care," Jack said, wrestling free from Arabella's grip.

"That was Captain Torrents, you idiot," Arabella said, slapping Jack upside the head. Jack looked blank.

"The infamous and the dreaded . . . ?" Arabella said.

"Not ringing any bells," Jack answered.

"The most notorious pirate this side of Hispaniola?" Arabella tried again.

"Oh, wait . . ." Jack said with a sudden look of recognition. Then his face fell again, "Nope. Sorry."

"Well, either way, you're as good as dead, stealing from him."

"Look, I am not a crook," Jack said. "This crummy sack here—and what's in it—is all I have. I would have brought more, but storage space for stowaways is very limited."

Arabella rolled her eyes.

"Then," Jack continued, "as is typical on this bloody island, a bloody pirate stole it from me. I don't even bloody remember it happening. The bloke, he got me from behind. But what I can tell you is that this here is my sack." Jack leapt onto an old barrel and opened the sack. "For instance," he said, digging around in the sack, then pulling out what looked like a stick of wax "this candle here is . . . not mine?" Jack looked at the candle, confused, then tossed it down.

"Surprise," Arabella said sarcastically.

"No, no, no!" Jack said, frustrated. Digging deeper, he pulled out what might have been old underwear. He shivered and tossed them away. After that came what looked like a dried up old rat.

"Arabella, by the way," the girl said. Jack did not look up. "The 'lassie' has a name," she continued, "and it's Arabella."

"Jack," Jack grunted, not really paying attention. There was no end to the horrible things in the sack. He threw out something that looked very much like petrified dung.

"Look, sorry I went wild on ye," Arabella said sincerely. "It's just, my father's temper is bad enough as it is. He's going to be in a frightful state now, spending the next week fixing up the place. Repairing the chairs and tables that ye helped destroy . . ."

There was a small thump as something Jack tossed hit Arabella square in the forehead. She caught it as it fell. It was a heavy coin.

"Thank you," she muttered sarcastically. "This makes up for everything."

"Well, it's the only thing in here worth anything," Jack said glumly. "My knife, my box, my stash of coins . . ." He looked up at her, bewildered, ". . . it's all gone."

Frustrated and angry, he turned the sack upside down and shook out several apple seeds.

Then something big and heavy fell out of the bottom, hitting the ground with a thunk. Jack leapt down to look at it. His eyes lit up as his fingers closed around smooth leather: a scabbard. A long scabbard. A sword, any sword, would fetch some nice cash on the black market . . . and this one looked like it had some history to it. He would be rich! Well, if not rich at least he could start to buy back the things he had lost.

Then again, perhaps he would keep it for himself. He didn't have a sword. And anyone who was anyone in the Caribbean had a sword. . . .

But as he picked up the scabbard, Jack realized

the weight was wrong: much too light to have a sword in it.

Jack groaned and threw the empty scabbard to the ground.

"Blasted pirates!"

He rubbed his eyes with his fingers and sank against the tavern wall, contemplating a bleak—and not-so-well-fed—future.

But Arabella's eyes widened as the scabbard tumbled to the ground. Was that a flash of gold?

She picked it up, ignoring Jack's grumbles, and turned it over in her hands. Although it was scratched and covered with dirt, glints of gold and silver still remained worked into the leather, which was sparkling with rain. And she could feel a design embossed on it.

"No, it couldn't be . . ." she breathed. "Get me some light," she ordered.

Normally Jack took orders from no one, least of all an angry tavern owner's daughter, but he heard something in Arabella's voice that caught his attention. Without protest, he took out a little flint-and-tinder kit from his coat pocket and lit the candle stub from the sack. Arabella took the candle and cast its weak light over the leather.

"Look, there—" she said, pointing at the scabbard. There were some words in a language neither of them recognized, abbreviations of some sort, and then some more inscriptions in Spanish. Below that was a strange image of a serpent with feathers, worked in reddish gold. Angular and foreign.

Quetzalcoatl. The Aztec god.

Arabella whistled. "Do ye know what this is?" she asked. Her voice quivered with excitement.

"Worth lots of gold?" Jack asked.

"It's the scabbard to the Sword of Cortés," she whispered.

Jack's eyes widened.

The adventure was about to begin . . .

Follow the continuing voyages of
Jack Sparrow in
Jack Sparrow and the Sword of Cortés